A Beginning-to-Read Book

Happy Hanukkah, Dear Dragon

by Margaret Hillert

Illustrated by David Schimmell

NORWOOD HOUSE PRESS

DEAR CAREGIVER, The *Beginning-to-Read* series is a carefully written collection of readers, many of which you may remember from your own childhood. This book, *Happy Hanukkah, Dear Dragon,* was written over 30 years after the first *Dear Dragon* books were published. The *New Dear Dragon* series features the same elements of the earlier books, such as text comprised of common sight words. These sight words provide your child with ample practice reading the words that appear most frequently in written text. The many additional details in the pictures enhance the story and offer the opportunity for you to help your child expand oral language skills and develop comprehension.

Begin by reading the story to your child, followed by letting him or her read familiar words and soon your child will be able to read the story independently. At each step of the way, be sure to praise your reader's efforts to build his or her confidence as an independent reader. Discuss the pictures and encourage your child to make connections between the story and his or her own life. At the end of the story, you will find reading activities and a word list that will help your child practice and strengthen beginning reading skills.

Above all, the most important part of the reading experience is to have fun and enjoy it!

Shannon Cannon

Shannon Cannon,
Literacy Consultant

Norwood House Press • P.O. Box 316598 • Chicago, Illinois 60631
For more information about Norwood House Press please visit our website at *www.norwoodhousepress.com* or call 866-565-2900.

Text copyright ©2008 by Margaret Hillert. Illustrations and cover design copyright ©2008 by Norwood House Press, Inc. All rights reserved. No part of this book may be reproduced or utilized in any form or by any means without written permission from the publisher.

Designer: The Design Lab

LIBRARY OF CONGRESS CATALOGING-IN-PUBLICATION DATA
    Hillert, Margaret.
      Happy Hanukkah, dear dragon / Margaret Hillert ; illustrated by David Schimmell.
        p. cm. — (A beginning-to-read book)
      Summary: "A boy and his pet dragon learn about Hanukkah from a Jewish friend"—Provided by publisher.
      ISBN-13: 978-1-59953-159-5 (library edition : alk. paper)
      ISBN-10: 1-59953-159-3 (library edition : alk. paper) [1.
    Dragons—Fiction. 2. Hanukkah—Fiction.] I. Schimmell, David, ill. II. Title.
    PZ7.H558Hat 2008
    [E]—dc22   2007037021

Manufactured in the United States of America

Come with me.
Come on. Come on.
Run, run, run.

Here is where we want to go.
Here is the house.
I want to see my friend.

Come in. Come in.
It is good to see you.
We can have fun.

Oh, I see something.
I see what you have on.
I do not have one.

No, you do not have one.
It is something for me
and my father.

But here is one for you.
Here at my house you can
have one.

And you can have one, too.
We want you to have it.

Come here.
Come here.
See what Mother can do.

Mother can make something.
Something good to eat.
You will see.

That looks good.
Is it for us?
Will we like it?

Yes. Yes.
It is for us.
One—and two—and three!
We will like it.

Now look at this.
See what I can do.

Oh, how pretty it is!
I like it.
I like it.

Now come with me.
I have something in here
that we can play with.

See what it is.
We can play with it.
We can have fun.

Now look here.
This is what you do.
This is how you make it go.

Oh, you are good at this!

Here is something for you.
Good, good, good.

Oh, I see what it is.
I can eat it.
It makes me happy.
But I have to go now.
I have to go to my house.

Look, Mother.
Look, Father.
See what I have.
It is something to play with.

Yes, we see it.
It looks like fun.
Fun to play with.

Here you are with me.
And here I am with you.
Oh, what a happy Hanukkah,
dear dragon.

READING REINFORCEMENT

The following activities support the findings of the National Reading Panel that determined the most effective components for reading instruction are: Phonemic Awareness, Phonics, Vocabulary, Fluency, and Text Comprehension.

Phonemic Awareness: Syllabication

Say the following words, clapping the syllables as you say them. Ask your child to tell you how many syllables are in each word:

happy-2	Hanukkah-3	dragon-2	dear-1	friend-1
something-2	festival-3	menorah-3	pretty-2	mother-2
latkes-2	party-2	gelt-1	celebrate-3	
holiday-3	dreidel-2	father-2	play-1	

Phonics: Syllabication

1. Explain to your child that the syllables in words with two consonants together are divided between the consonants. Write the following words on separate index cards:

happy (hap-py)	shopping (shop-ping)	pretty (pret-ty)
mommy (mom-my)	little (lit-tle)	apple (ap-ple)
puddle (pud-dle)	rattle (rat-tle)	bubble (bub-ble)
wiggle (wig-gle)	supper (sup-per)	middle (mid-dle)
skinny (skin-ny)	supply (sup-ply)	daddy (dad-dy)
puzzle (puz-zle)	wrapping (wrap-ping)	

2. Ask your child to cut (for younger children, ask them to draw a line for you to cut along) the words apart based on the syllables that are divided between the two consonants.

3. Mix the separated word parts up, and help your child put them together to make words.

Vocabulary: Hanukkah Words

1. On a blank sheet of paper, make four squares by folding the paper in half twice. Write each of the following story words in one of the squares (at the top or bottom, leaving space for a picture): menorah, yarmulke, gelt, dreidel.

2. Read each word aloud and ask your child to repeat the words. Ask your child to find the pages in the book where each of the objects is featured.

3. Discuss the story and pictures to help your child understand what each of the Hanukkah objects is.

A menorah is a special holder for eight candles, plus one candle to light the others, used in Jewish worship.

The cap worn by Jewish males is called a yarmulke.

Dreidel is a top that children spin to play a popular Hanukkah game.

Gelt is a Yiddish term for money. Jewish children receive gold foil-wrapped chocolate coins for Hanukkah.

4. Ask your child to illustrate each square.

Fluency: Shared Reading

1. Reread the story to your child at least two more times while your child tracks the print by running a finger under the words as they are read. Ask your child to read the words he or she knows with you.

2. Reread the story taking turns, alternating readers between sentences or pages.

Text Comprehension: Discussion Time

1. Ask your child to retell the sequence of events in the story.

2. To check comprehension, ask your child the following questions:
   - What is the name of the holiday in this story?
   - What is your favorite part of the story? Why?
   - If your family celebrates Hanukkah ask: What do we do to celebrate Hanukkah?
   - If your family does not celebrate Hanukkah ask: What special celebrations do we have in the winter? What do we do to celebrate?

WORD LIST

Happy Hanukkah, Dear Dragon **uses the 61 words listed below.** This list can be used to practice reading the words that appear in the text. You may wish to write the words on index cards and use them to help your child build automatic word recognition. Regular practice with these words will enhance your child's fluency in reading connected text.

a	Father	I	oh	us
am	for	in	on	
and	friend	is	one	want
are	fun	it		we
at			play	what
	go	like	pretty	where
but	good	look(s)		with
			run	will
can	Hanukkah	make		
come	happy	me	see	yes
	have	Mother	something	you
dear	here	my		
do	house		that	
dragon	how	no	three	
		not	the	
eat		now	this	
			to	
			too	
			two	

ABOUT THE AUTHOR Margaret Hillert has written over 80 books for children who are just learning to read. Her books have been translated into many different languages and over a million children throughout the world have read her books. She first started writing poetry as a child and has continued to write for children and adults throughout her life. A first grade teacher for 34 years, Margaret is now retired from teaching and lives in Michigan where she likes to write, take walks in the morning, and care for her three cats.

Photograph by Glenna Washburn

ABOUT THE ADVISER Shannon Cannon contributed the activities pages that appear in this book. Shannon serves as a literacy consultant and provides staff development to help improve reading instruction. She is a frequent presenter at educational conferences and workshops. Prior to this she worked as an elementary school teacher and as president of a curriculum publishing company.